Where's Curly?

Heather Amery

Illustrated by Stephen Cartwright

Edited by Jenny Tyler

This is Curly. He lives at Apple Tree Farm.

There is a little yellow duck in every picture. Can you find it?

This is Poppy and Sam.
They are looking for Curly the pig.

Poppy and Sam look around
the farm for Curly.

Poppy and Sam go to the haystack.

I can't see Curly.

Poppy and Sam walk across the farmyard.

What's making that noise?

Poppy and Sam look everywhere.

Poppy and Sam go to the woodshed.

Mrs. Boot, Poppy and Sam stop at the apple shed.